THIS PUFFIN MODERN CLASSIC
BELONGS TO

_____

For
Elizabeth Attenborough

Some reviews for *Please Mrs Butler*

Other books by Allan Ahlberg

Poetry and Jokes
Friendly Matches
The Ha Ha Bonk Book
Heard it in the Playground
The Mighty Slide

Fiction for younger readers
The Happy Families series

Older Fiction
The Bear Nobody Wanted
The Better Brown Stories
The Giant Baby
The Improbable Cat
Jeremiah in the Dark Woods
My Brother's Ghost
Ten in a Bed
Woof!

Picture Books
with Janet Ahlberg
The Baby's Catalogue
Burglar Bill
Bye Bye Baby
Cops and Robbers
Each Peach Pear Plum
Funnybones
It Was a Dark and Stormy Night
The Jolly Postman
The Jolly Christmas Postman
The Jolly Pocket Postman
Peepo!
Starting School

with André Amstutz
The Fast Dog Slow Fox series

with Raymond Briggs
The Adventures of Bert
A Bit More Bert

with Fritz Wegner
The Little Cat Baby

Please Mrs Butler

ALLAN AHLBERG

Illustrated by Fritz Wegner

PUFFIN BOOKS

PUFFIN BOOKS

Published by the Penguin Group
Penguin Books Ltd, 80 Strand, London WC2R 0RL, England
Penguin Putnam Inc., 375 Hudson Street, New York, New York 10014, USA
Penguin Books Australia Ltd, 250 Camberwell Road, Camberwell, Victoria 3124, Australia
Penguin Books Canada Ltd, 10 Alcorn Avenue, Toronto, Ontario, Canada M4V 3B2
Penguin Books India (P) Ltd, 11 Community Centre, Panchsheel Park, New Delhi – 110 017, India
Penguin Books (NZ) Ltd, Cnr Rosedale and Airborne Roads, Albany, Auckland, New Zealand
Penguin Books (South Africa) (Pty) Ltd, 24 Sturdee Avenue, Rosebank 2196, South Africa

Penguin Books Ltd, Registered Offices: 80 Strand, London WC2R 0RL, England

www.penguin.com

First published by Kestrel Books 1983
Published in Puffin Books 1984
Published in Puffin Modern Classics 2003
5

Copyright © Allan Ahlberg, 1983
Illustrations copyright © Fritz Wegner, 1983
Introduction copyright © Julia Eccleshare, 2003
All rights reserved

Set in Century Schoolbook

Made and printed in England by Clays Ltd, St Ives plc

British Library Cataloguing in Publication Data
A CIP catalogue record for this book is available from the British Library

ISBN 0–141–31458–3

www.greenpenguin.co.uk

Penguin Books is committed to a sustainable future
for our business, our readers and our planet.
The book in your hands is made from paper
certified by the Forest Stewardship Council.

Introduction

by Julia Eccleshare

Puffin Modern Classics series editor

Allan Ahlberg likes school and, as a former teacher, he knows a lot about it. In these kindly and witty poems, he reveals all the best and worst details of both classroom and playground – and revels in them. The ignominy when it comes to being chosen last for a team in 'Picking Teams' and the potential shame that might be brought about by the visit of the school nurse on one of her regular nit searches in 'School Nurse' are just two of the embarrassing moments almost everyone has experienced and which Allan Ahlberg lightly portrays. Then there's the full range and ridiculousness of the myriad excuses that are offered for not doing homework as relayed in 'Excuses' while, in a completely contrasting mood and most poignantly, he highlights the enveloping gloom of the struggling reader in 'Slow Reader'.

But it's not just how school seems to pupils that concerns Allan Ahlberg. Without ever speaking down to the real audience, he also captures the feelings of the teachers, with whom adult readers are bound to sympathize.

Allan Ahlberg has an exceptional ability to take you right back to the classroom and playground – and it may not always be easy to escape. There are endless projects to be finished, tricks to be played on unsuspecting supply teachers and a list of missing things that seems to be growing longer.

Whatever the subject – even 'Slow Reader' – all the poems are injected with a refreshingly positive attitude and, as a result, *Please Mrs Butler* makes school a place of creativity and fun.

Contents

SCHOOL TIME

Please Mrs Butler	2
Back to School	4
Slow Reader	5
There's a Fish Tank	6
Supply Teacher	8
Emma Hackett's Newsbook	10
Who Knows?	12
Blame	14
Glenis	15
The School Nurse	16
Small Quarrel	18
Headmaster's Hymn	20
As I was Coming to School	21

PLAY TIME

Complaint	24
Swops	26
Picking Teams	27
If I Wasn't Me	28
I Did a Bad Thing Once	30
Old Joke	31
The Gang	32

DINNER TIME

When I was Young	36
Sometimes God	38
It is a Puzzle	40

Dog in the Playground   42

SCHOOL TIME AGAIN
Scissors   48
The Cane   50
Excuses   53
Eating in Class   54
Reading Test   55
Colin   56
Only Snow   58
The Runners   60
The Ordeal of Robin Hood   61
Do a Project   68
Lost   70
School is Great   72
Now the Day is Over   73

HOME TIME
Balls on the Roof   76
The Challenge   78
Our Mother   80
Haircut   81
Is That Your Apple?   82
Scabs   83
Bedtime   85

SCHOOL TIME

Please Mrs Butler

Please Mrs Butler
This boy Derek Drew
Keeps copying my work, Miss.
What shall I do?

Go and sit in the hall, dear.
Go and sit in the sink.
Take your books on the roof, my lamb.
Do whatever you think.

Please Mrs Butler
This boy Derek Drew
Keeps taking my rubber, Miss.
What shall I do?

Keep it in your hand, dear.
Hide it up your vest.
Swallow it if you like, my love.
Do what you think best.

Please Mrs Butler
This boy Derek Drew
Keeps calling me rude names, Miss.
What shall I do?

Lock yourself in the cupboard, dear.
Run away to sea.
Do whatever you can, my flower.
But *don't ask me!*

Back to School

In the last week of the holidays
I was feeling glum.
I could hardly wait for school to start;
Neither could mum.

Now we've been back a week,
I could do with a breather.
I can hardly wait for the holidays;
Teacher can't either.

Slow Reader

I – am – in – the – slow
read – ers – group – my – broth
er – is – in – the – foot
ball – team – my – sis – ter
is – a – ser – ver – my
lit – tle – broth – er – was
a – wise – man – in – the
in – fants – christ – mas – play
I – am – in – the – slow
read – ers – group – that – is
all – I – am – in – I
hate – it.

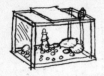

There's a Fish Tank

There's a fish tank
In our class
With no fish in it;
A guinea-pig cage
With no guinea-pig in it;
A formicarium
With no ants in it;
And according to Miss Hodge
Some of our heads
Are empty too.

There's a stock-cupboard
With no stock,
Flowerpots without flowers,
Plimsolls without owners,
And me without a friend
For a week
While he goes on holiday.

There's a girl
With no front teeth,
And a boy with hardly any hair
Having had it cut.
There are sums without answers,
Paintings unfinished,
And projects with no hope
Of ever coming to an end.
According to Miss Hodge
The only thing that's brim-full
In our class
Is the waste-paper basket.

Supply Teacher

Here is the rule for what to do
Whenever your teacher has the flu,
Or for some other reason takes to her bed
And a different teacher comes instead.

When this visiting teacher hangs up her hat,
Writes the date on the board, does this or that,
Always remember, you must say this:
'*Our* teacher never does that, Miss!'

When you want to change places or wander about,
Or feel like getting the guinea-pig out,
Never forget, the message is this:
'*Our* teacher always lets us, Miss!'

Then, when your teacher returns next day
And complains about the paint or clay,
Remember these words, you just say this:
'That *other* teacher told us to, Miss!'

Emma Hackett's Newsbook

Last night my mum
Got really mad
And threw a jam tart
At my dad.
Dad lost his temper
Then with mother,
Threw one at her
And hit my brother.
My brother thought
It was my sister,
Threw two at her
But somehow missed her.
My sister,
She is only three,
Hurled four at him
And one at me!

I said I wouldn't
Stand for that,
Aimed one at her
And hit the cat.
The cat jumped up
Like he'd been shot,
And landed
In the baby's cot.
The baby –
Quietly sucking his thumb –
Then started howling
For my mum.
At which my mum
Got *really* mad,
And threw a Swiss roll
At my dad.

Who Knows?

I know
Something you don't know.

No, you don't,
I know it.

You don't know it.
How could you know it!
Nobody knows it,
Only me.

I just know it.

Prove it, then.
Tell me what I know.

Tell yourself.
Why should I tell you?
You're the one
Who knows it.

Yes, but you *don't* know it!

You prove it.

I can't prove it.
How can I prove it?
If I tell you what I know
You'll say you know it already.

I do know it already.

Well, *you* prove it.

No, I can't prove it.
If I tell you what I know
You know,
You'll change it to something else.

No, I won't.
If you tell me
What you know I know,
I'll know if you know it.

Yes, but I *won't* know!

That's all right.
Then I'll know
Something you don't know.

Blame

Graham, look at Maureen's leg,
She says you tried to tattoo it!
I did, Miss, yes – with my biro,
But Jonathan told me to do it.

Graham, look at Peter's sock,
It's got a burn-hole through it!
It was just an experiment, Miss, with the lens.
Jonathan told me to do it.

Alice's bag is stuck to the floor,
Look, Graham, did you glue it?
Yes, but I never thought it would work,
And Jonathan told me to do it.

Jonathan, what's all this I hear
About you and Graham Prewitt?
Well, Miss, it's really more his fault:
He *tells* me to tell him to do it!

Glenis

The teacher says:

Why is it, Glenis,
Please answer me this,
The only time
You ever stop talking in class
Is if I ask you
Where's the Khyber Pass?
Or when was the Battle of Waterloo?
Or what is nine times three?
Or how do you spell
Mississippi?
Why is it, Glenis,
The only time you are silent
Is when I ask you a question?

And Glenis says:

The School Nurse

We're lining up to see the nurse
And in my opinion there's nothing worse.
It is the thing I always dread.
Supposing I've got *nits* in my head.

I go inside and sit on the chair.
She ruffles her fingers in my hair.
I feel my face getting hot and red.
Supposing she finds *nits* in my head.

It's taking ages; it must be bad.
Oh, how shall I tell my mum and dad?
I'd rather see the dentist instead
Than be the one with *nits* in his head.

Then she taps my arm and says, 'Next please!'
And I'm out in the corridor's cooling breeze.
Yet still I can feel that sense of dread.
Supposing she *had* found nits in my head.

Small Quarrel

She didn't call for me as she usually does.
I shared my crisps with someone else.

I sat with someone else in assembly.
She gave me a funny look coming out.

I put a pencil mark on her maths book.
She put a felt pen mark on mine.

She moved my ruler an inch.
I moved hers a centimetre.

I just touched her PE bag with my foot.
She put the smallest tip of her tongue out.

She dipped her paint brush in my yellow.
I washed mine in her paint water.

She did something too small to tell what it was.
I *pretended* to do something.

I walked home with her as usual.
She came to my house for tea.

Headmaster's Hymn

(to be sung)

When a knight won his spurs
In the stories of old,
He was – *'Face the front, David Briggs,*
What have you been told?'
With a shield on his arm
And a lance in his – *'Hey!*
Is that a ball I can see?
Put – it – a – way.'

No charger have I
And – *'No talking back there.*
You're supposed to be singing,
Not combing your hair.'
Though back into storyland
Giants have – *'Roy,*
This isn't the playground,
Stop pushing that boy!'

Let faith be my shield
And – *'Who's eating sweets here?*
I'm ashamed of you, Marion,
It's not like you dear.'
And let me set free
With – *'Please stop that, Paul King.*
This is no place for whistlers,
We'd rather you sing!'

As I was Coming to School

As I was coming to school, Sir,
To learn my ABC,
I was picked up and put in a sack, Sir,
And carried off on his back, Sir,
By a Russian who took me to sea.

So I had to swim all the way back, Sir,
And I still had my legs in the sack, Sir,
And the waves they were forty foot high, Sir,
Which is really the reason why, Sir –
I would not tell a lie, Sir –
I'm late for school today.

Is it all right to go out to play?

PLAY TIME

Complaint

The teachers all sit in the staffroom.
The teachers all drink tea.
The teachers all smoke cigarettes
As cosy as can be.

We have to go out at playtime
Unless we bring a note
Or it's tipping down with rain
Or we haven't got a coat.

We have to go out at playtime
Whether we like it or not.
And freeze to death if it's freezing
And boil to death if it's hot.

The teachers can sit in the staffroom
And have a cosy chat.
We have to go out at playtime;
Where's the fairness in that?

Swops

I'll give you
A penny chew
A plastic whistle
A pot of glue
A suck of sherbet
A small canoe
A piece of string
A cockatoo
A bag of crisps
And a kangaroo!

For your Milky Way.
What do you say?

No.

Picking Teams

When we pick teams in the playground,
Whatever the game might be,
There's always somebody left till last
And usually it's me.

I stand there looking hopeful
And tapping myself on the chest,
But the captains pick the others first,
Starting, of course, with the best.

Maybe if teams were sometimes picked
Starting with the worst,
Once in his life a boy like me
Could end up being first!

If I Wasn't Me

If I wasn't me,
I'd rather be
Batman or (second choice) Robin.

I'd come to school
In the batmobile,
Friends in the back,
Me at the wheel.

The teacher would say, 'Batman?'
And I'd say, 'Here, Miss.'

If I wasn't me,
I'd rather be
Wonderwoman's daughter.

I'd wear a cloak
With fancy shorts,
And win every race
In the school sports.

The teacher would say, 'Thanks, Wondergirl!'
And mum would win the Mothers' Race.

I Did a Bad Thing Once

I did a bad thing once.
I took this money from my mother's purse
For bubble gum.
What made it worse,
She bought me some
For being good, while I'd been vice versa
So to speak – that made it worser.

Old Joke

'Look at your hands!'
The teacher cried.
'Couldn't be dirtier
If you tried.
What would you say
If mine were like this?'
'We'd be too polite
To mention it, Miss!'

The Gang

1st boy: Who wants to be in my gang?
2nd boy: Who else have you got?
1st boy: Well really just me at the moment.
2nd boy: That's not a lot.

2nd boy: Who wants to be in his gang?
3rd boy: I do – me!
2nd boy: Right, he's boss, I'm second-in-command,
           You're number three.

3rd boy: Who wants to be in our gang?
Line up at the den.
We've got the three leaders already,
We need a few men.

1st boy: Who wants to be in their gang?
Don't spread it about.
I've stopped being boss of it now.
They voted me out.

1st boy: Who wants to be in my gang?

DINNER TIME

When I was Young

When I was young and had no sense,
I used to lie in a crib.
I used to sleep for hours and hours
And dribble on my bib.

I had no sense when I was young.
I sat in a high chair
And spooned my dinner from the plate
And threw it everywhere.

I could not talk when I was young.
I could not catch a ball.
I only sucked the books I had,
I didn't *read* at all.

When I was young and had no sense,
I used to lie in a crib.
I used to sleep for hours and hours
And dribble on my bib.

Sometimes God

Sometimes when I'm in trouble,
Like if Gary Hubble
And his gang
Are going to get me and beat me up,
Or I'm outside Mr Baggot's door
Waiting to have the slipper for pour-
Ing paint water in Glenis Parker's shoe,
This is what I do:
I ask for help from God.

Get me out of this, God,
I say.
I'll behave myself, then –
Every day.

Sometimes when I'm really
Scared, like once when I nearly
Got bit by this horse,
Or the other
Week when Russell Tucker's brother
Was going to beat me up
For throwing Russell Tucker's PE bag
On the boiler-house roof, or Roy
And me got caught in the toi-
Lets by Mr Baggot turning all the taps on
And he said,
I've had enough of boys like you,
This is what I do:
I ask for help from God.

Stop this happening, God,
I say.
I'll believe in You then –
Every day.

And it works . . . sometimes.

It is a Puzzle

My friend
Is not my friend anymore.
She has secrets from me
And goes about with Tracy Hackett.

I would
Like to get her back,
Only do not want to say so.
So I pretend
To have secrets from her
And go about with Alice Banks.

But what bothers me is,
Maybe *she* is pretending
And would like *me* back,
Only does not want to say so.

In which case
Maybe it bothers her
That *I* am pretending.

But if we are both pretending,
Then really we are friends
And do not know it.

On the other hand,
How can we be friends
And have secrets from each other
And go about with other people?

My friend
Is not my friend anymore,
Unless she is pretending.
I cannot think what to do.
It is a puzzle.

Dog in the Playground

Dog in the playground
Suddenly there.
Smile on his face,
Tail in the air.

Dog in the playground
Bit of a fuss:
I know that dog –
Lives next to us!

Dog in the playground:
Oh, no he don't.
He'll come with me,
You see if he won't.

The word gets round;
The crowd gets bigger.
His name's Bob.
It ain't – it's Trigger.

They call him Archie!
They call him Frank!
Lives by the Fish Shop!
Lives up the Bank!
Who told you that?
Pipe down! Shut up!
I know that dog
Since he was a pup.

Dog in the playground:
We'll catch him, Miss.
Leave it to us.
Just watch this!

Dog in the playground
What a to-do!
Thirty-five children,
Caretaker too,
Chasing the dog,
Chasing each other.
I know that dog –
He's our dog's brother!

We've cornered him now;
He can't get away.
Told you we'd catch him,
Robert and – Hey!
Don't open that door –
Oh, Glenis, you fool!
Look, Miss, what's happened:
Dog in the school.

Dog in the classroom,
Dog in the hall,
Dog in the toilets –
He's paying a call!
Forty-six children,
Caretaker too,
Headmaster, three teachers,
Hullabaloo!

Lost him! Can't find him!
He's vanished! And then:
Look, Miss, he's back
In the playground again.

Shouting and shoving –
I'll give you what for! –
Sixty-five children
Head for the door.

Dog in the playground,
Smile on his face,
Tail in the air,
Winning the race.

Dog in his element
Off at a jog,
Out of the gates:
Wish I was a dog.

Dog in the playground:
Couldn't he run?

Dog in the playground
        . . . Gone!

SCHOOL TIME AGAIN

Scissors

Nobody leave the room.
Everyone listen to me.
We had ten pairs of scissors
At half-past two,
And now there's only three.

Seven pairs of scissors
Disappeared from sight.
Not one of you leaves
Till we find them.
We can stop here all night!

Scissors don't lose themselves,
Melt away or explode.
Scissors have not got
Legs of their own
To go running off up the road.

We really need those scissors,
That's what makes me mad.
If it was seven pairs
Of children we'd lost,
It wouldn't be so bad.

I don't want to hear excuses.
Don't anyone speak.
Just ransack this room
Till we find them,
Or we'll stop here . . . all week!

The Cane

The teacher
had some thin springy sticks
for making kites.

Reminds me
of the old days, he said;
and swished one.

The children
near his desk laughed nervously,
and pushed closer.

A cheeky girl
held out her cheeky hand.
Go on, Sir!

said her friends.
Give her the stick, she's always
playing up!

The teacher
paused, then did as he was told.
Just a tap.

Oh, Sir!
We're going to tell on you,
The children said.

Other children
left their seats and crowded round
the teacher's desk.

Other hands
went out. Making kites was soon
forgotten.

My turn next!
He's had one go already!
That's not fair!

Soon the teacher,
to save himself from the crush,
called a halt.

(It was
either that or use the cane
for real.)

Reluctantly,
the children did as they were told
and sat down.

If you behave
yourselves, the teacher said,
I'll cane you later.

Excuses

I've writ on the wrong page, Miss.
My pencil went all blunt.
My book was upside-down, Miss.
My book was back to front.

My margin's gone all crooked, Miss.
I've smudged mine with my scarf.
I've rubbed a hole in the paper, Miss.
My ruler's broke in half.

My work's blew out the window, Miss.
My work's fell in the bin.
The leg's dropped off my chair, Miss.
The ceiling's coming in.

I've ate a poison apple, Miss.
I've held a poison pen!
I think I'm being *kidnapped*, Miss!
So . . . can we start again?

Eating in Class

Little girl
Box of paints
Sucked her brush
Joined the saints.

Little boy
Bubble gum
Blew himself
To kingdom come.

reading test

tree	little	milk	egg	book
read	ing	test	I	took
school	sit	frog	playing	bun
it	was	not	much	fun
flower	road	clock	train	light
still	I	got	it	right
picture	think	summer	peo . . .	
			popple . . .	
			peep . . .	
			pe . . .	
			p . . . well, nearly.	

Peo...Popple
Peep..pe.........p

55

Colin

When you frown at me like that, Colin,
And wave your arm in the air,
I know just what you're going to say:
'Please, Sir, it isn't fair!'

It isn't fair
On the football field
If their team scores a goal.
It isn't fair
In a cricket match
Unless you bat *and* bowl.

When you scowl at me that way, Colin,
And mutter and slam your chair,
I always know what's coming next:
'Please, Sir, it isn't fair!'

It isn't fair
When I give you a job.
It isn't fair when I don't.
If I keep you in
It isn't fair.
If you're told to go out, you won't.

When heads bow low in assembly
And the whole school's saying a prayer,
I can guess what's on your mind, Colin:
'Our Father . . . it isn't fair!'

It wasn't fair
In the Infants.
It isn't fair now.
It won't be fair
At the Comprehensive
(For first years, anyhow).

When your life reaches its end, Colin,
Though I doubt if I'll be there,
I can picture the words on the gravestone now.
They'll say: IT IS NOT FAIR.

Only Snow

Outside, the sky was almost brown.
The clouds were hanging low.
Then all of a sudden it happened:
The air was full of snow.

The children rushed to the windows.
The teacher let them go,
Though she teased them for their foolishness.
After all, it was only snow.

It was only snow that was falling,
Only out of the sky,
Only on to the turning earth
Before the blink of an eye.

What else could it do from up there,
But fall in the usual way?
It was only *weather*, really.
What else could you say?

The teacher sat at her desk
Putting ticks in a little row,
While the children stared through steamy glass
At the only snow.

The Runners

We're hopeless at racing,
Me and my friend.
I'm slow at the start,
She's slow at the end.

She has the stitch,
I get sore feet,
And neither one of us
Cares to compete.

But co-operation's
A different case.
You should see us
In the three-legged race!

The Ordeal of Robin Hood

There is a new boy in our class;
He came the other day.
He hadn't any friends, of course,
So we let him be in our play.

That was the first mistake we made.

The play was called 'Bold Robin Hood';
We'd practised it all week.
The new boy missed rehearsals
So he had no lines to speak.

He thought of a few, though, as you will see.

Besides, this boy was foreign,
His English wasn't good.
He said his name was Janek;
He'd not heard of Robin Hood.

Robin Hood didn't get to Poland, Miss Hodge said.

Well, first we pushed the desks back
To make a bigger space.
Then we hung this curtain up
For the outlaws' hiding place.

Miss Hodge just let us get on with it.

Little John   Friar Tuck   Robin Hood   Sheriff of Nottingham   Guard

Kevin Jukes was Robin Hood,
Roy was Little John,
I was the Sheriff of Nottingham –
I had this red cloak on.

The new boy was one of my guards, supposedly.

The swords we had were rulers;
The cupboard, Robin's den;
And most of us had moustaches
Drawn with black felt pen.

Roy's was navy blue, but you could hardly tell.

The rest of the class sat round to watch,
Miss Hodge was watching too.
Then Keith announced the title
And who was playing who.

*Keith was also Friar Tuck with a cushion
up his coat.*

At first it all went pretty well,
Mistakes we made were slight;
The trouble only started
When we got to the first fight.

There should have been three fights altogether;
should have been.

What we'd practised was an ambush
To rescue Friar Tuck,
With me and my guards just riding by
Until the outlaws struck.

No horses, of course, just 'clip-clop' noises.

So there was I, my cloak tossed back,
Duelling with Robin Hood;
While Janek – I didn't know it then –
Was guarding me more than he should.

Perhaps there's nothing in the Polish language
for 'Aaargh!'

Guards, you see, are meant to fight
For a little while, then lose.
Get captured, killed or wounded,
Whatever way they choose.

Usually our plays had guns in them, only this
time Miss Hodge said she was sick of guns.

But Janek wasn't having that,
He wouldn't even defend;
And the way he was generally carrying on,
The play would never end.

*That was the second mistake we made: it ended
all right.*

And still the worst was yet to come
In Robin Hood's ordeal:
Not only wouldn't Janek die,
He was sword-fighting for real!

*The Merrie Men were looking less merry by the
minute.*

Will Scarlett's hand was stinging
From the blows that Janek smote,
And Friar Tuck was thankful
For that cushion up his coat.

*Alan-a-Dale and Little John were already
behind the curtain.*

We did our best to stop him;
Tried 'whispering' in his ear;
But he was shouting foreign words,
We couldn't make him hear.

*I could see then how Poland knocked us out of
the World Cup.*

The play was going haywire now,
The audience could tell.
When some of the guards tried changing sides,
Janek polished them off as well.

'Pole-ished' – get it? Keith thought of that on the way home.

Then, having done for the outlaws,
He shoved me out of the way
And had a go at Robin Hood.
That wasn't part of the play!

In my opinion, Miss Hodge should have stopped it then.

Now Kevin had this plastic sword
(The play was his idea)
And being who he was, of course,
Was supposed to show no fear.

I was showing fear, and Janek was on my side.

But once the sword was broke in half,
And minus his Merrie Men,
Robin Hood dropped the other half
And surrendered there and then.

*Then Miss Hodge stopped it, which I thought
was a bit late.*

Anyway, that was the end of that.
The audience gave us a clap.
Me and Roy took the curtain down
And joined the rush for the tap.

*It's thirsty work, acting; and we had our
moustaches to wash off.*

Roy also fetched the first-aid box,
Put a plaster on his shin,
And offered to settle Kevin's nerves
With a junior aspirin.

*Kevin was worried what his mum was going to
say about the sword.*

Janek, meanwhile, was prowling round
With *his* sword still in his hand;
Suspecting another ambush, perhaps,
From another outlaw band.

Miss Hodge said he reminded her of Errol Flynn,
whoever he was.

Keith said, let's wait for the Christmas play
And have Janek in again.
He'd make mincemeat of the shepherds,
And slaughter the Three Wise Men.

He'd be worse than Herod, Keith said.

But I'm about fed up with plays;
Football's a better bet.
Now we've got this match against Class 4
And we've never beaten them yet.

You can probably guess what was in my mind;
Roy could.

So tomorrow Janek brings his kit
(The kick-off's half-past three);
And we'll play him in the forward line:
He's a striker . . . obviously.

Do a Project

Do a project on dinosaurs.
Do a project on sport.
Do a project on the Empire State Building,
The Eiffel Tower,
The Blackpool Tower,
The top of a bus.

Ride a project on horses.
Suck a project on sweets.
Play a project on the piano.
Chop a project on trees
Down.

Write a project on paper,
A plaster cast,
The back of an envelope,
The head of a pin.

Write a project on the Great Wall of China,
Hadrian's Wall,
The playground wall,
Mrs Wall.

Do a project in pencil,
In ink,
In half an hour,
In bed,
Instead
of something else,
In verse,
Or worse;
Do a project in playtime.

Do a project on your hands and knees,
Your head,
With one arm tied behind you.

Do a project wearing handcuffs,
In a steel coffin,
Eighty feet down
At the bottom of the Hudson River
(Which ideally should be frozen over),
On Houdini.

Forget a project on Memory;
And refuse one on Obedience.

Lost

Dear Mrs Butler, this is just a note
About our Raymond's coat
Which he came home without last night,
So I thought I'd better write.

He was minus his scarf as well, I regret
To say; and his grandma is most upset
As she knitted it and it's pure
Wool. You'll appreciate her feelings, I'm sure.

Also, his swimming towel has gone
Out of his PE bag, he says, and one
Of his socks, too – it's purplish and green
With a darn in the heel. His sister Jean

Has a pair very similar. And while
I remember, is there news yet of those fairisle
Gloves which Raymond lost that time
After the visit to the pantomime?

Well, I think that's all. I will close now,
Best wishes, yours sincerely, Maureen Howe
(Mrs). P.S. I did once write before
About his father's hat that Raymond wore

In the school play and later could not find,
But got no reply. Still, never mind,
Raymond tells me now he might have lost the note,
Or left it in the pocket of his coat.

School is Great

When I'm at home, I just can't wait
To get to school – I think it's great!

Assemblies I could do without,
But I love it, giving hymn-books out.

Writing's fun, when you try each letter,
But sharpening the pencils first – that's better!

Football leaves me with the stitch,
But I'd miss my playtime to mark the pitch.

Cooking cakes gives you a thrill,
But cleaning the bowl out's better still.

Story's nice at the end of the day,
But I'd rather empty the rubbish away.

Yes, school's great – though I'll tell you what:
Going-home-time beats the lot!

Now the Day is Over

Now the day is over
'I won six marbles from Glen;
I'm going to play him again!'
Night is drawing nigh
'My boy-friend's either Jeremy Coathe
Or Kevin Jukes – or both!'
Shadows of the evening
'I've gone and lost the back-door key;
Mother'll murder me!'
Steal across the sky.
A – men.
'Come on, Glen;
I'll play you again!'

HOME TIME

Balls on the Roof

The caretaker went on the roof today,
The first time for years.
He put his ladder against the wall
And cleared the guttering.

Some of the children stayed to watch;
It was after school.
He threw the balls down that he found
And they caught them.

That guttering was a graveyard for balls.
Balls with moss on them.
Balls you couldn't even buy any more.
Balls too old to bounce.

There was a sorbo ball with R.T. on it,
Not Russell Tucker's –
Raymond Tate's – he'd left – ages ago!
Gone to the Comp.

There was a ball so perished and worn,
It was like Aero.
I could've kicked that up, the caretaker said,
When I was a boy.

The children studied each relic as it came down,
But made no notes.
They said, we're taking that mossed-up one
For the Nature Table.

The caretaker cleared the guttering.
He put his ladder away.
And the children kicked the least un-bouncy ball
In the empty playground.

The Challenge

My dad can fight your dad.
You must be mad!

My mum can fight your mum.
No chance, chum.

My brother can fight your brother.
Pull the other!

My gran can fight your gran.
You're joking, man!

My cat can fight your cat.
Don't bet on that.

And *I* can fight *you*.
. . . Toodle-oo!

Our Mother

Our mother is a detective.
She is a great finder of clues.
She found the mud and grass on our shoes,
When we were told not to go in the park –
Because it would be getting dark –
But come straight home.

She found the jam on our thumbs,
And in our beds the tiniest crumbs
From the cakes we said we had not eaten.
When we blamed the cat for breaking the fruit
    bowl –
Because we did not want any fuss –
She *knew* it was us.

Haircut

I hate having my hair cut;
And when it's done,
I hate going to school next day
And being *told* about it –
By everyone.

'Oh, you've had your hair cut,' they say.
'Oh, you should wear a hat!'
'Oh, you've had a *bare*-cut,' they say.
And silly things like that.

I can stand having my hair cut,
Though I'd rather let it grow.
What I can't stand
Is being *told* I've had it cut –
As if I didn't know!

Is That Your Apple?

Is that your apple?
What a charming sight!
I would be your best friend
For a little bite.

We could play at my house.
You could stay to tea.
We could get my train-set out.
We could watch TV.

We could go up to the park.
We could sail my yacht.
We could . . . Oh, you greedy pig,
You've gone and ate the lot.

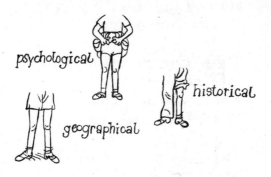

psychological

geographical

historical

Scabs

The scab on Jean's knee
Is geographical.
Bexhill-on-Sea:
Tripped up on school trip.

The scab on Henry's knee
Is historical.
Oldest scab in Class Three:
Second year sack race.

The scab on Paul's knee
Is pugilistical.
Fighting Clive Key:
He got a cut lip.

The scab on Sally's knee
Is psychological.
Hurts if she does PE:
Painless at playtime.

The scab on Brian's knee
Is bibliographical.
Fooling around in library:
Banged into bookcase.

The scabs on the twins' knees
Are identical.
Likewise the remedies:
Hankies and spit.

The scab on Eric's knee
Is economical.
£2.50:
Second-hand skates.

The scab on Debby's knee
Is diabolical.
Nothing to see:
Hurts like the devil.

Bedtime

When I go upstairs to bed,
I usually give a loud cough.
This is to scare The Monster off.

When I come to my room,
I usually slam the door right back.
This is to squash The Man in Black
Who sometimes hides there.

Nor do I walk to the bed,
But usually run and jump instead.
This is to stop The Hand –
Which is under there all right –
From grabbing my ankles.

The End